A CHRISTMAS CAROL

Written by Penny Dolan

Illustrated by Karen Donnelly

D0227283

1 Scrooge hears a warning

It was Christmas Eve and everyone was hurrying home.

Mr Scrooge stayed on in his cold, gloomy office, adding up how much money people owed him.

Bob Cratchit, Scrooge's helper, had to work too, but he longed to go home.

Just then, Scrooge's nephew Fred popped into the office. "Hello, Uncle," he said cheerfully, "will you come round for Christmas tomorrow?"

Scrooge scowled. "No! Christmas is a waste of time," he grumbled. "Go away! You too, Cratchit."

Scrooge went home, his footsteps echoing along the cold, empty streets. As he approached his gloomy house, a dreadful figure appeared from the fog. It was ghostly white and had dark, hollow eyes.

Scrooge stared. "It can't be," he stammered. It reminded him of his old friend, Marley. But Marley was dead.

As Scrooge went inside, his front door slammed shut behind him. He was so scared that he ran up to his room and lit every candle.

Suddenly the clocks rang out, on and on, but then Scrooge heard something far worse. Iron chains were rattling up the stairs, closer and closer. A terrible ghost entered, dragging a metal chest full of rusty money. It *was* Marley's ghost!

"I'm here to warn you, Scrooge," he howled.
"Three strange ghosts will visit you tonight.
Look and listen or it'll be the worse for you."

With a terrible cry, Marley's ghost disappeared.
Scrooge dived into bed and pulled the covers
up tightly.

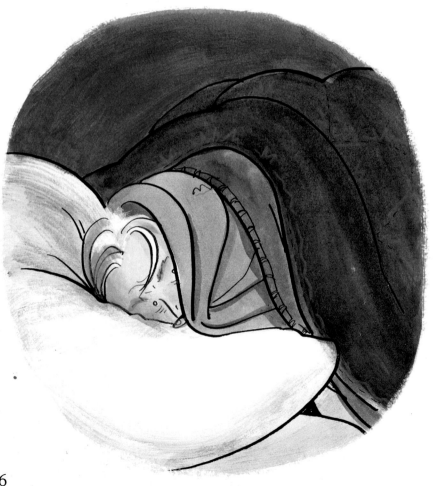

2 Scrooge travels back in time

At midnight, a glowing figure in a long white robe appeared.

"I'm the Ghost of Christmas Past!" He took Scrooge's hand. "I'm taking you back in time."

Scrooge shook from head to foot, but he remembered Marley's warning. He held on tightly as the ghost flew out into the night sky.

When the clouds parted, Scrooge saw snowy
hills and fields and a small village.

"I remember that place," he gasped.
"I lived there long ago." A lonely little boy stood
shivering by a tree. "Oh! I know that unhappy
child," Scrooge cried sadly. "It's me!"

They flew onwards to a cold, empty school.
The same boy sat there all alone.

"I was sent away to that cruel place," Scrooge said,
"where it was never Christmas."

Suddenly a laughing girl ran into the school.

"Brother, you're coming home right now!" she cried, hugging him. "The coach is waiting outside."

"My sister was always so kind to me," Scrooge said, as they soared off through the clouds.

"Are you always kind to her son, Fred?" the ghost asked.

Scrooge knew he was not.

Then the clouds parted again showing a Christmas
party where young people were having fun.
Scrooge saw himself among them, a happy young man.

"I had friends then," he moaned, "but I've none now.
I spent my time keeping my money, not my friends."
A tear ran down his cheek.

"That was your past," said the ghost, disappearing.

Scrooge was back in his room again, sad and alone.

⌒ 3 Scrooge learns about Christmas ⌒

Before Scrooge got back into bed, a dazzling ghost appeared.

"Scrooge, I am the Ghost of Christmas Present. It's time for you to learn how people enjoy Christmas. Come!"

The ghost led him off to the next room.
Scrooge stared. It couldn't be his house because
there were decorations everywhere and the room
was full of good things to eat and drink. There, in
the middle of this gigantic feast, sat a huge man
with a white beard and a furry robe.

"It's Father Christmas!" Scrooge whispered, but before he could say another word, the cheery feast disappeared. The ghost took his hand and led him out into the city. Scrooge saw happy people everywhere, but nobody saw him.

15

They came to a poor home. "Look inside," said the ghost. Scrooge saw Bob Cratchit and his family around their Christmas dinner table.

Bob held up a glass. "Three cheers for us!" he cried merrily. "And one cheer for poor Mr Scrooge."

"Poor?" said his wife. "How can he be poor?"

"He is poor, my dear. Scrooge's money doesn't make him feel as rich as I do with you all around me."

Everyone clapped and then the smallest child, Tiny Tim, sang them a sweet carol. Scrooge felt so alone.

The ghost led Scrooge on through the streets.
People were celebrating Christmas everywhere.

They came to a house where a family party
was going on.

"It's Fred's home!" Scrooge cried.

There was Fred, with his wife and friends
and children, all laughing and playing games.

Scrooge remembered turning down Fred's invitation
and immediately felt sadder than before.

As they left Fred's home, the ghost pointed. "Look. You've one last thing to see."

There, in an alley, crouched a pair of hungry, ragged children. Scrooge was horrified by the hate in their eyes.

"Beware!" said the ghost. "Those who are starved and treated badly may never learn to be kind. Remember that!"

The ghost led Scrooge back to his cold house and left him alone in the darkness.

Scrooge shrank down in his armchair, shaking.
Suddenly another terrifying ghost appeared,
wrapped in a long black cloak and holding out
one bony hand.

"I am the Ghost of Christmas Future, Scrooge,"
it said, "and I'll show you what's to come."
Away they floated into the fog. "Listen!"

Scrooge heard low voices talking about someone who'd died.

"That man! He was the meanest person I ever knew. I won't miss him," said one voice.

"He never helped anyone, did he?" said another.

"Never ever. Don't even want to remember his name," said a third. The others agreed.

"I know those voices," thought Scrooge, "but who are they talking about?"

"You'll find out soon enough," answered the ghost. "Come!" It took Scrooge onwards through the fog.

"You've seen this home before," it said. "But time has changed things. The small boy became ill and died."

Scrooge saw the Cratchit family weeping around Tiny Tim's empty chair.

"Everywhere I look I seem to see that dear boy," sighed Mrs Cratchit.

Bob gave a sad smile. "We'll never ever forget him. He gave us so many happy memories."

"Oh no!" Scrooge thought. "I can't believe it – and my money might have helped him," he sobbed.

Suddenly a cold wind blew the fog away and they were standing in a gloomy graveyard.

"Look!" The ghost pointed to a lonely, forgotten grave.

Scrooge saw his own name on the grave.

"I'm the person they were talking about, the one nobody wants to remember." He fell to his knees, shaking. "Ghost," he begged, "is this truly the future? Or have I got time to change things?"

But the dreadful ghost turned into dust.

⌒ 5 Scrooge on Christmas Day ⌒

Scrooge woke up in his own bed, still trembling.

"But I'm alive," he said, "and it's Christmas morning and there's no time to lose!" Laughing, he jumped out of bed and into his best clothes.

Scrooge ran to the shops, bought a huge basket of food and took it round to Bob Cratchit's home. When Bob and his family saw the gift, their eyes lit up.

"Merry Christmas," said Scrooge, secretly giving Bob an envelope full of extra pay. "From now on, I promise I'll help you all."

"Hooray!" cheered Tiny Tim.

Then Scrooge walked around wishing everyone a merry Christmas until he reached his nephew's front door.

"Happy Christmas, Fred!" Scrooge said, smiling very cheerfully.

Fred beamed with surprise. "Welcome, Uncle Scrooge. You'll have Christmas dinner here, after all?"

"I will," laughed Scrooge, delighted. "Thank you, dear Fred."

That Christmas was the happiest day Scrooge had ever spent.

From that moment, he changed and before long Scrooge was known for bringing kindness and joy to all, especially at Christmas.

Scrooge and the three ghosts

Ideas for reading

Written by Clare Dowdall BA(Ed), MA(Ed)
Lecturer and Primary Literacy Consultant

Learning objectives: read independently and with increasing fluency longer and less familiar texts; draw together ideas and information from across a whole text; give some reasons why things happen or characters change; explore how particular words are used, including words and expressions with similar meanings; engage with books through exploring and enacting interpretations

Curriculum links: Citizenship: Choices, History: What was it like to live here in the past?

Interest words: Scrooge, echoing, cruel, dazzling, gigantic, ragged, dreadful

Word count: 1,273

Resources: whiteboard, internet, books about the Victorian era

Getting started

- Ask children if they know the famous story *A Christmas Carol* by Charles Dickens, or if they have seen a film version of it. Explain that it was written over 150 years ago and that they are going to read a shortened version that is written for children.

- Show children the front cover. Ask them to predict what sort of story it might be and when it was set, e.g. a ghost story set in the past.

- Read the blurb with the children. Ask them to suggest why Scrooge was not a kind man and how they think Scrooge might change through the story. Write the ideas on a whiteboard for children to refer to later.

Reading and responding

- Read Chapter 1 together. Check children understand that Scrooge has been visited by a ghost, and that he has been told that he will be visited by three more strange ghosts that night.

- Draw children's attention to the use of powerful vocabulary, e.g. *dreadful* (p4), *stammered*, (p4), *howled* (p6). Discuss how this vocabulary helps to paint a picture in the reader's mind and creates an atmosphere of tension and fear.